Dear mouse friends,
welcome to the world of

Geronimo Stilton

The Editorial Staff of
The Rodent's Gazette

1. Linda Thinslice
2. Sweetie Cheesetriangle
3. Ratella Redfur
4. Soya Mousehao
5. Cheesita de la Pampa
6. Mouseanna Mousetti
7. Yale Youngmouse
8. Toni Tinypaw
9. Tina Spicytail
10. Maximilian Mousemower
11. Valerie Vole
12. Trap Stilton
13. Branwen Musclemouse
14. Zeppola Zap
15. Merenguita Gingermouse
16. Ratsy O'Shea
17. Rodentrick Roundrat
18. Teddy von Muffler
19. Thea Stilton
20. Erronea Misprint
21. Pinky Pick
22. Ya-ya O'Cheddar
23. Mousella MacMouser
24. Kreamy O'Cheddar
25. Blasco Tabasco
26. Toffie Sugarsweet
27. Tylerat Truemouse
28. Larry Keys
29. Michael Mouse
30. Geronimo Stilton
31. Benjamin Stilton
32. Briette Finerat
33. Raclette Finerat

Geronimo Stilton
A learned and brainy
mouse; editor of
The Rodent's Gazette

Thea Stilton
Geronimo's sister and
special correspondent at
The Rodent's Gazette

Trap Stilton
An awful joker;
Geronimo's cousin and
owner of the store
Cheap Junk for Less

Benjamin Stilton
A sweet and loving
nine-year-old mouse;
Geronimo's favorite
nephew

WE WANT STIL-TON!

What a rat's nest this morning in front of my office! When I came up from the subway, I saw **mice** of all **shapes and sizes** packing the street. All their snouts were in the air. They were staring at the windows of my office! The crowd began to chant:

"STIL-TON! STIL-TON! WE WANT STIL-TON! GERO-NIMO STIL-TON!"

Uh-oh. I had a feeling these mice weren't looking for my autograph.

Luckily, no one recognized me.

Because, you see, *I* am Geronimo Stilton!

Quiet as a mouse, I wriggled through the crowd and sneaked up the back stairs. I dashed into my office, huffing and puffing for air. I really needed to get back to my gym, Rats La Lanne. My secretary, Mousella, ran to meet me. "*Mr. Stilton!* Horrible news!" she squEAKed, waving the phone book we had just printed. "New Mouse City's YELLOW PAGES are a disaster! There isn't one correct phone number! Not one!"

Pale as a slice of mozzarella cheese, I leafed through the book. "Addresses . . . telephone numbers . . .

they're all wrong? *I am ruuuuuined!*" I
SHRIEKED, pulling at my whiskers.

I heard the crowd yelling and leaned out
my window. They had lit a huge bonfire
right in the middle of the street. They
were **BURNING** my directories!!!

A fierce-looking mouse pointed at
me with his paw. "That's him!
That's Geronimo Stilton! The one
who published the Yellow
Pages! He's the one who's
turned New Mouse City on its
tail!"

The crowd began chanting
again. **"STIL-TON! STIL-TON!
WE WANT STIL-TON!"**

Suddenly, all the telephones in my office
started RINGING. I answered the phone on
my desk.

"I need to speak with that cheddarface, *Mr. Stilton!* " an angry voice snarled on the other end.

"Um, Mr. Stilton isn't here," I squeaked in a high-pitched voice. Hopefully, the caller wouldn't know it was me. "I don't know where he is," I continued. "He might be in the hospital with an ingrown toenail. Or maybe he's helping out down at the Creaky Mouse Nursing Home. He does a lot of charity work, you know."

I decided to unplug the telephones, but the fax machines were all spitting out nasty letters. Threatening e-mails popped up on my computer screen: **"We know where you live! You can't hide! No hole is safe!"**

Mousella wrung her paws. Tears rolled down her snout. *"Mr. Stilton*, this is a total disaster! Even our own telephone number is wrong!" she squeaked. "We are now the **Furry Tails** Toilet Paper Company!"

"Don't worry, Mousella. I have everything under control," I cried, closing my eyes. Maybe I was just having a *bad dream*. I waited a few seconds, then opened my eyes. The rodents outside were throwing moldy cheese balls at my window.

No, this wasn't a *bad dream*. It was a living **NIGHTMARE!**

WHAT A FURBRAIN!

knock knock

Just then, Blunders, my editor in chief, **knocked** at the door.

"*Mr. Stilton*, your cousin Trap is here," he announced, tripping over his tail.

"I am not in for anyone!" I shouted.

Blunders jumped, spilling his mug of cheddar tea. "Um, well, he says it's urgent!"

"I — am — not — in!" I repeated.

Next thing I knew, my cousin, a **plumpish** mouse with **BEADY EYES,**

was standing before me. He put both paws on my desk and smiled.

Have you ever met my cousin? He owns a shop in downtown New Mouse City—Cheap Junk for Less. He's a **terrible prankster**. And his favorite hobby is teasing me! Another thing you should know about Trap, he's like a refrigerator magnet for trouble. Sometimes you can't tear those two apart!

"What do you want? Can't you see I am busy?" I yelled. "And please, take your paws off my desk!"

"**Hello, there,** Cousinkins! What's up?" he squeaked, picking his teeth with my letter opener.

I took off my glasses so that I could cry freely. "Can't you see I am in big trouble here?" I choked. "Oh, why did I choose this job? I could have been a lifeguard down at WaterRat Park or a waiter at The Cheese Garden. . . ."

Trap smirked. "Are you kidding? A *furbrain* like you couldn't do those jobs!"

"I am not a furbrain!" I squ**EAK**ed, fuming.

Just then, the phone *ring!* **rang**. In a flash, Trap *ring!* had his paw on the receiver. *ring!*

"If it's for me, please tell them I am not in," I begged.

He picked up the phone and straightened his tie. "Hello, this is *The Stilton Publishing Company*. No, *Mr. Stilton* is not in. Yes, yes, I agree that he is a hopeless cheddarface, a total nincompoop!" my cousin nodded. "Well, of course I will tell him. He is a complete *furbrain*! Thank you for calling!" he added before hanging up.

I twisted my whiskers in rage. Steam

poured out from my ears. I felt like a cheddar cheese marshmallow left in a microwave too long.

"I asked you to say I was not in," I shrieked. "I didn't say make friends with any wacky mouse who calls!"

"That wasn't any wacky mouse!" my

cousin insisted. "I was talking to Saucy Le Paws, the famous chef. He says you switched the number of his restaurant with the one for the city dump! I'd better not tell you where he said he wanted to send you."

All of a sudden, my cousin's eyes lit up. "Hey, that reminds me. Do you know why I'm here?"

I put my head in my paws. "Yes, I do," I mumbled. "You are here to drive me nuts! And it's working. I'm packing my bags for the Mad Mouse Center. I'll leave tonight."

"Not so fast," Trap said, giggling. "I am here to get you out of this mess! Just listen to my brilliant idea. . . ."

I groaned. Not another one of my cousin's brilliant ideas! The last time I'd gotten involved in one of his crazy schemes, I'd

ended up stuck in a spooky castle in
Transratania!

Saucy Le Paws

THE MOST WANTED MOUSE

Trap's latest brilliant idea came from a **TELEVISION** show.

"I saw this great show last night. It was one of those real-life mysteries," he began. "It took place in the *southern seas*, near the *Claw Islands*. Someone had

spotted an island all covered in silver! And unlike most islands, this one seems to be moving! We should go looking for it!"

"Not on your life!" I shrieked. "You know I *HATE* traveling."

Trap gave me a SLY smile. "Just think about it. A little disappearing act might be good for you," he advised. "Did you know the Viking Rats football team is lined up outside? They haven't looked this angry

since they lost the Super Mouse Bowl. Plus, the mayor has put you on the Most Wanted list. I passed ten policemice on my way here. One was sharpening his teeth with a cheese shredder!

"Besides, think about the mysterious island," he murmured. "My whiskers are standing on end just thinking about all that silver! Thea and Benjamin have already agreed to come."

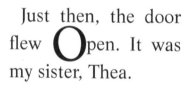

Just then, the door flew Open. It was my sister, Thea.

"Do you know that the YELLOW PAGES are all wrong?" she squeaked. "I just called the

GRAND CHEDDAR HOTEL to book a weekend with my new sweetie pie. I got Ratcatraz Prison instead. They offered me two rooms with a view of the barbed wire fence!"

I couldn't help but giggle. My sister goes through sweetie pies the way a starving rat goes through a plate of nachos!

"It's not funny, furbrain!" my sister scolded me.

Suddenly, a messenger mouse rushed in with the **SIX** cups of warm milk and the soothing yoga tape I had just ordered.

"Um, *Mr. Stilton*," he interrupted. "Did you know you've switched the number for *PIZZA MOUSE* with the one for BENT WHISKERS MEMORIAL? Last night, I ordered a pizza and got an ambulance instead. The

hospital wants to sue you for damages!"

Just then, my young nephew Benjamin raced through the door. "Uncle, Uncle, I have to tell you something **very important!**" he cried. "I checked your phone book, and it's full of mistakes! My school is getting lots of calls asking for a tattoo parlor. Uncle, do you think I should get a tattoo? By the way, the principal said he wants to speak with you."

I closed my eyes and counted the holes in a slice of Swiss. Then I stood up. "All right! You win!" I told Trap. "Let's go! Now!"

WE LEAVE AT DAWN

Next morning at dawn, I met everyone on the beach. Trap was bent over a pump trying to blow up a **huge balloon**. It was **purple** with **yellow dots**.

"What on earth is this? Where did you find it?" I shrieked.

"It's a hot-air balloon. I got it real cheap at the flea market," my cousin replied cheerfully.

I rolled my eyes. "I don't see why we have

to travel in a hot-air balloon. And why did you pick such a horrible color? It looks like a giant prune with freckles!" To be honest, I was a little worried. It didn't seem like the safest way to travel. But Thea was already busy fixing a hole in the basket.

Benjamin posed in front of the balloon. "Uncle, would you take my picture?" he asked, grinning from ear to ear.

Half an hour later, we took off in the **balloon**. I sat at the bottom of the basket and began writing in my diary. *6:25 A.M., we have just left the beach at*

New Mouse City. We are headed west for the Claw Islands.

Day after day, I wrote down everything that happened in my journal. I figured writing would take my mind off traveling. Did I mention how much I hate to travel?

Finally, at noon on the eleventh day, we caught sight of the Claw Islands. Trap jumped up and down as if he had just won the Mouse Lotto.

"The silver island should be somewhere around here! Keep your eyes peeled!" he shouted. "You, too, *Gerry Berry*. Although with your eyes you'd probably have trouble seeing Santa Mouse on his sleigh!"

"I have excellent eyesight with my glasses on!" I CRIED, glaring at my cousin.

Minutes later, I was the first to spot the

I was the first to spot the island.

island. So much for my bad eyes! I cleaned my glasses to get a clearer view. A dot of silver swayed back and forth with the waves. It was the island, all right!

"Look over there!" I shouted with excitement.

But then something totally strange happened. Zing! A cannonball flew by just above my ears!

Zinnng! Zinng!

Two more cannonballs brushed by our balloon.

Somehow I had a sinking feeling things were about to get worse.

I really do HATE traveling.

THE SILVER CLAW

Thea grabbed the binoculars.

"Who is firing at us?" cried my sister. "Cheese niblets! That's not an island. It's a pirate ship. And those are cats!"

"Cats?" we all squeaked, terrified. Then another shot shredded our **balloon**. Down we went. We held on to the basket of the balloon for dear life as we hit the water.

"Thea, Benjamin, Trap . . . are you still alive?" I whispered. I paddled desperately, trying to stay afloat.

A lifeboat was approaching. A large black-and-white cat stood at the front.

"Faster, faster, you fools!" he meowed to the cats pulling the oars.

Soon the boat pulled up beside us. The big cat plucked us out of the water.

"Mice!" he cried gleefully. "How *purr*fect!"

Licking their whiskers, the pirates threw us into the lifeboat and rowed us back to their ship. It was called The Silver Claw. Except for the *black sails*, the whole ship was covered in polished silver. It shone brightly under the sun.

THREE CHEERS FOR THE BLACK BANDIT!

The nasty cat who had captured us was pushing us down a hallway. He stopped now and then to prick our tails with the point of his sword.

"Forward, you rodents!" he commanded. "You must pay your respects to His Excellency, Prince of All Pirates, Grand Duke of Deadly Deeds, Earl of Evil Matters, and let's not forget Baron of Broken Bones . . . the one and only Black Bandit!" He meowed solemnly.

My cousin put his paws on his hips. "So this prince character is your boss?" he scoffed. "Sounds like he needs to pick one name and stick with it! For your information, my name is **TRAP:**

T as in TAKE THAT, YOU CRAZY CAT!

R as in RUN FOR YOUR LIFE!

A as in ATTENTION, EVERYONE: HERE I COME!

P as in PAWS OFF IF YOU WANT TO LIVE!

The cat sneered. "The Black Bandit will soon wipe that grin off your snout," he told my cousin. Trap just yawned and looked bored. He was a braver mouse than I. I was quaking in my Mouse Jordans! Meanwhile, we had reached an enormous dining room.

Black Bandit

More than one hundred cats were stuffing their furry faces with food. At the head of the table sat a black cat. His fur was as black as a mouse hole at night. His long whiskers were dusted with golden powder. He wore a cape of **black** silk and a large black hat with a golden feather on top. His shiny boots were decorated with buckles that jingled at his every step. In short, he was the most terrifying creature I'd ever laid eyes on. But it got worse. Under his belt he carried a razor-sharp sword. And even scarier than *that* was the cat's right paw. It was a horrifying silver hook!

Prince speared an apple, threw it in the air, and cut it up with his sword. Then he caught it in midair with his silver hook.

"Three cheers for the Black Bandit! Hip, hip, meow!"

"Three cheers for Prince, three cheers for the **Black Bandit**!" the cats roared as one. "Hip, hip, meow! Hip, hip, meow! Hip, hip, meow!"

With a *grunt* of approval, the **Black Bandit** sat down in his armchair. Then he noticed us.

The other cats stood up. "Mice! Mice!" they purred, licking their whiskers.

The **Black Bandit** stared straight into my eyes. One of his eyes was yellow and the other was green. It gave me the creeps. Like the time I met that circus mouse with two tails.

"Silence!" the **Bandit** *cried*, waving his hook in the air.

Everyone was silent. He lifted my chin with his sharp claw.

"Well, well, well," he *hissed* in a grim

THREE CHEERS FOR THE BLACK BANDIT!

voice. "What do we have here?"

I *coughed*. His breath smelled worse than a bucket of moldy cheese!

Suddenly, a tomcat dressed in bright yellow leaped into the air and raced over to a jar full of pickled snails. Then he began giggling like a kitten on his first trip to the fish market. There was a **crazy** look in his eyes.

NO MORE SNAILS!

It was Prowls, the Black Bandit's brother.

"Mice at last! No more snails!" he meowed.

"*Keep quiet, you nitwit!*" snapped the Bandit. Then he turned to us.

"Four **plump** mice," he murmured.

He looked down at his sharp claws as if he were longing for a nail file. Then he glanced at a cat in an apron who was huffing and puffing in the corner. He was busy roasting a long rod of snails over a fire.

"So tell me, where are you from?" asked the **Bandit**, curling his tail into a question mark.

Just then, Prowls began dancing around the room in a whirl of yellow. He stopped in front of Trap and pricked him with his sword. "What's wrong? Cat got your tongue?"

I glanced at my cousin. He was snorting like Scar Rat, the famous boxer, before a big match. "If you were on our island, you wouldn't have a tongue!" Trap shrieked.

"Jumping tuna fish!" cried the Black Bandit. "Do you mean you are from Mouse Island? Our ship has been searching for ages for that place! It sounds amazing!"

"Amaaaaazzzing!" echoed the other cats.

"Amaaaaazzzzing!" shouted Prowls. He was out of beat with the other cats.

Prowls

"Pipe down, you ninny!" raged the Bandit, crushing his brother's tail with the heel of his boot.

"Meeeeowwww!" cried Prowls.

The Bandit brushed Prowls's fur off his boot. Once again he turned toward us. "So, tell us where your island is. We will take you back immediately," he purred.

"Oh, we don't want to go back," I said, pretending not to care.

"And why not?" asked the Bandit, narrowing his eyes.

"Well, you see, the four of us are the only survivors of a terrible sickness," I whispered, thinking quickly. We had to stop these bandit cats from finding Mouse Island! "Yes, acutis FUNGUS MOUSitiS, a very contagious disease, has wiped out the whole population! So we left, hoping to find another island of rodents." I wiped away a fake tear.

A greasy cat began playing a violin.

The **Black Bandit** scratched his head with one long claw.

"So there are no mice on the island?" he mumbled, **Drumming** the table with his claws.

Meanwhile, a greasy cat began *playing a violin*.

"What would Your Excellency like to hear?" he asked, slimy as melted cheddar. "'The Ballad of the Killer Cat'? Or 'The Dance of the Pouncing Paws'?"

But the **Bandit** only had eyes for us. "That's enough, Patches! Enough playing for today!" he growled. Then he signaled for me to step closer.

"Come on," he hissed. "Are you telling

me **a little lie**, or are you pulling my paw?"

I stayed quiet. All the cheese in the world couldn't make this mouse squeak!

The Bandit's eyes drilled into mine. Then he let out a loud, evil laugh.

"Get me Chef Slobbertooth!" he yelled.

MICE WITH SPICE!

Just then, the doors of the kitchen FL E W OP E N.

A big cat wearing a cook's hat decorated with a skull and crossbones bounded in.

"Your Meowing Majesty, weren't the stuffed snails to your liking? I wish I could do more for Your Whiskered Excellency, but I —" he began.

But the Bandit held up his paw. "Enough jabbering!" he ordered. "Tell me, what do you think of these rodents?"

"Mice!" screeched Slobbertooth, nearly jumping out of his fur. "My favorite meal to prepare! What an honor, Your Royal Purrfection! What a privilege! What a —"

The **Black Bandit** clawed the air. "Silence!" he shrieked. "Tell me their breed and the best way to cook them."

Slobbertooth pulled out a magnifying glass and studied us. Thea patted her head modestly. "Oh, Mr. Tooth, dear," she said with a wink. "Don't be too **cruel**. I'm having a bad fur day."

For a minute, Slobbertooth smiled, confused. Leave it to my sister to charm the claws off a cat!

"Yes, well, these mice are healthy specimens," said the chef, pulling himself together. "It wouldn't be a bad idea to **fatten them** up, though. We could feed them for a week before eating them."

First course...

"How many servings can you dish out?" asked the Bandit.

Slobbertooth twirled his whiskers, deep in thought.

Second course...

"I'd say about twenty," he finally answered. He picked up a thick cookbook. I peeked at the cover. It was the latest edition of *Cooking for Cats: From Rodents to Sweet Rolls* by Kitty Carver.

Third course...

"Let's see, I could bake them in a stew with some juicy vegetables," he suggested. "Or a squeaky mouse dip is

always delicious. Then again, there's the *classic:* roast mouse. And, of course, nothing beats my mouse bone steak with pepper and lemon."

Licking his lips, the Black Bandit nodded. "Yes, the last recipe will be just *purr*fect," he decided. "But don't use too much garlic. We don't want to hide the sweet taste of rodent meat!"

"Of course, Your Highness. You couldn't have made a better choice," crooned Slobbertooth. "Yes siree, you are clearly an expert on the subject of food."

The **Black Bandit** ignored the compliments. He waved the cook back toward the kitchen. "Out of my sight!" he growled, giving him a boot.

"**AT YOUR ORDERS**, Your Most High and Excellent Claws!" muttered Slobbertooth, bowing low. I waited for him to kiss the **Bandit's** boots. But he didn't. I guess even Slobbertooth wasn't up to that much slobbering. He raced out of the room.

The **Black Bandit** turned to the cat who had captured us. He threw him the ring he wore on his little finger. "*Take this, you idiot.* This is my reward for your brave deed!" he said.

"Thank you, Excellency. You are more than generous," **STAMMERED** the cat. He bowed so low his whiskers brushed the floor. Then he slunk away.

The Bandit jumped onto the table. "Take the rodents to their cells, and woe to the cat who lets them escape!" he meowed fiercely. He slashed the air with his sword. All the pirates disappeared under the table to avoid having their whiskers chopped off.

Four big, ugly cats sprang into action. They looked like they had been pro wrestlers in one of their nine lives. They pushed us up a stairway leading to the Cat's Ear, a very tall silver tower.

"Check this one out! He's plump enough to eat raw!" roared a striped cat, feeling Trap's tail.

"Raw, my paw!" squeaked my cousin. "Don't even think about touching me!"

"**Hee! Hee! Hee!** I'm not going to bite . . . at least not yet!" sniggered the cat. He pushed us into a dark cell. The key turned in the lock behind us.

We looked at one another in a daze. We were doomed to be devoured by cats! **WHat a Horrible Way to go.**

I just *knew* something bad was going to happen, even before we left.

Traveling really is the *pits*!

The cats were lowering the sails.

THE CAT'S EAR

I stared out the window of our prison cell in the Cat's Ear. The cats were lowering the sails so they could change direction.

"Rotten, stinking cats!" I muttered, gripping the bars with my paws.

"Holey cheese! I don't want to end up in a *pot to be cooked* by that sleazy Slobberface," sobbed my cousin. "I don't even like PEPPER. It makes my fur break out in hives." He sniffled, then blew his nose loudly into a **big yellow handkerchief with red dots**.

Benjamin grabbed the sleeve of my jacket. "Uncle, I think maybe —" he began.

"Benjamin, please, we'll talk about it later," I said. I patted him on the head.

"Auntie, I think maybe —" my nephew tried, pulling my sister's paw.

"Benjamin, be a **good mouse**! Can't you see we're talking about serious matters?" said Thea.

"Why don't you go play with some fur

balls or something," suggested Trap.

"But I have a plan!" squEAKed Benjamin, annoyed.

"A *plaaaan*?" we cried.

"Why didn't you say so?" said Trap.

Benjamin sighed. "Well, I got this plan from a book I read. It's called SCRAM! MY LIFE ON THE RUN by Fearless Frank the Adventure Mouse," he explained. "Fearless Frank was stuck in a prison cell just like this one. He tied a rope to one of the bars and hung outside the window. When the jailer found the cell empty, he ran off to get help. Fearless Frank climbed back into the cell and escaped through the open door."

Trap scratched his head. "But how are we going to fit through the bars?" he asked. "We'll need to cut through them somehow."

Benjamin began to dig through his pockets. He pulled out three sticks of cheddar-flavored bubble gum, a glow-in-the-dark yo-yo, and . . . a Swiss army knife! He opened it, and a small file popped out.

"Do you remember this, Uncle Geronimo? You gave it to me for my birthday. I take it with me wherever I go," squeaked my nephew.

"This is great!" shouted Trap.

"We'll take turns filing the bars," said Thea. "One of us will have to keep watch. But . . . what about the noise?" She twirled her whiskers, deep in thought.

Two minutes later, my sister jumped up, clapping her paws. "I've got it!' she cried.

"We will sing!"

RAH! RAH! RATS!

We decided that Benjamin should keep watch while Trap worked away at the bars. To drown out the noise, Thea and I began singing at the top of our lungs. I must admit I never knew my sister had such a voice. She was truly awful! She sounded as if her tail were stuck in Slobbertooth's high-speed blender!

First we sang the ever-popular "Mouse Island March." As any rodent knows, it goes like this:

"We are *mice*, hear us squeak.
Our *hearts* are strong.
We are *never* weak . . ."

Then we sang another oldie but goodie. It was New Mouse City's fight song, "Rats with Bats":

"We are *rats* with bats.
We are **brave and true**.
So stand back, all you cats,
Rah! Rah! *Rats* are coming through!"

After a few more battle songs, we moved on to some more recent tunes. Thea wiggled her tail to "Nibbling in the Rain." Benjamin joined in on "Squeak Goes the Hamster" and "If You're Happy and You Know It, Clap Your Paws."

All of a sudden, Benjamin started squeaking. **CLAWS**, our jailer cat, was on his way.

"Well, well, what's going on here?" Claws meowed, squinting at us.

"We are singing to cheer ourselves up," I explained, looking very sad. "We have given up all hope. You cats are much too smart for us!"

Claws grinned. "Good, I like to see a mouse who knows when he's beat. I mean, everyone knows cats have **bigger** brains than mice," he laughed. "That should make us twice as smart, right? Hey, want to hear me count to ten?" Before we knew it, Claws was off and counting. He only got stuck twice, on five and nine.

When he was done, we all applauded. I tried not to clap too hard — I was afraid he'd start on the alphabet. Luckily, Claws just bowed. "OK, Micey," he giggled, "go ahead and sing your songs. But no sad songs, please. I don't want the other cats to see me crying."

What a softie! He was beginning to grow on me a little. If only he wasn't a cat . . .

"Whatever you say, Boss," squeaked **TRAP**, with a smirk.

We were almost ready for our escape.

THE HEART OF A COURAGEOUS MOUSE

The night before our escape, I could not sleep. I missed my comfy bed at home. I missed my bright cheddar-colored sheets. I missed my great-aunt Ratsy's cozy comforter. "Just another reason to **HATE** traveling," I sighed to myself, tossing and turning. Moonlight filled the room. I stared at the wall. It was then that I saw the silver drawing inscribed there.

"Slimy Swiss Balls!!" I yelled, waking up Thea. "It's a plan of this ship," I whispered. I quickly made a copy of the drawing in my diary.

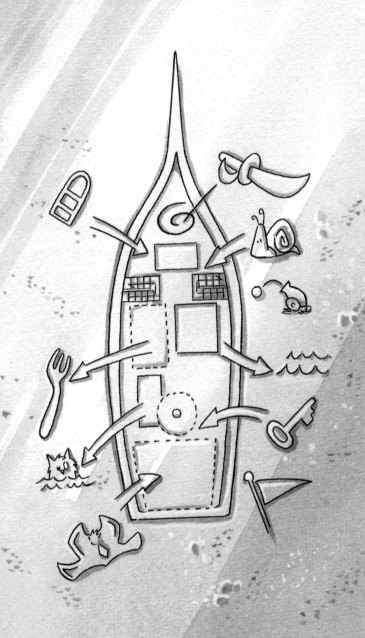

I saw the silver drawing.

"This will help us escape," I explained. "Now we'll know exactly how to get around this monster-sized ship. See, this is one of Slobbertooth's kitchens, here is Whiskers's Lounge and Pool Room, and there are the Cozytime Catnap Quarters. I wonder who drew this plan on the wall."

"Maybe a prisoner," whispered my sister, stroking the drawing. "Look, there is a date and a message here. It says

1663."

I peered closer. The message was written in Squeakeeze, the ancient language spoken long ago on Mouse Island. I read it aloud:

"THE HEART OF A COURAGEOUS MOUSE SHALL ALWAYS BE FREE. RODENTS, BE SMART, FOLLOW YOUR HEART!"

SNAIL PUDDING

Trap had been yakking it up with **CLAWS**, the cat guarding us. That is how he found out why the pirate cats did not eat fish. It seemed that the **Black Bandit** was allergic! In fact, the very sight of fish was enough to give him a terrible itch. So they ate only snails!

"Yes, it's an awful shame," Claws sighed. "All those yummy fishies swimming right below us in the ocean. Even *they* know the **Black Bandit** will not let us touch them. They call us 'fraidy cats. The other day two kid tunas even tried sunbathing on our deck. They looked so tasty. Of course, *he* made us throw them back. 'If I cannot eat fish, then *NO ONE* else can!' the *Bandit* told us." Claws groaned. "So it's snails, snails, and more snails!"

The morning we were to be cooked finally came. Claws arrived, *jingling* his keys.

"Hey, there, my little rodents!" he called. "The chef will soon be here to take charge of you. While you wait, how about *A LITTLE SNACK*? Just think of it as your final **fattening**. Eat, drink, and be tasty!" He collapsed in a fit of giggles.

"OK, get ready," my cousin whispered to us. Then he strolled over to Claws.

"You know, Claws, I would just love a slice of snail tart," he began. "And could you put some snail pudding on the side? You do have snail pudding, don't you?"

CLAWS grinned. "Of course we do, dear friend!" he meowed. "And I'll bring you a delicious side of *snail slime* that will make your fur curl!" He skipped off to the kitchen, twirling his tail behind him.

As soon as he left, Thea grabbed the blankets and tied them together to make a rope. I ran to the window and pulled out the

bar we had filed. Then I lowered myself out the window. The others followed.

We lined up alongside the **silver** tower, holding on for dear life. I couldn't stop myself from peeking at the ground. The drop made my head spin. The cannons below looked like toy weapons, and the cats looked like furry little ants.

We lined up alongside the tower, holding on for dear life.

We waited for just a few minutes, but it felt like forever. I checked to see if my fur had turned gray. Suddenly, a NASTY SMELL drifted out the window. It was the hot snail pudding. After another minute, we heard a furious meowing.

"Well, lock me up in a room filled with bloodhounds and throw away the key!" shrieked Claws. "Those squeaky, rotten mice tricked me!"

"Rats!" yelled Twitch, the night watchcat, running toward the window.

"Someone will lose his tail because of this!" hissed Pounce, the head jailer.

MEOW! MEOW!

Just then, an earsplitting meowing made our fur stand on end. It was the cats' **alarm** siren!

Me e e e o o o o o w w W W W W W W **!!**

All the pirates ran out on deck. The hallway was empty.

Quiet as mice, we climbed up the rope and dropped back into our cell. The door was open. Not a cat in sight! We hid in the suits of armor that lined the hall. Seconds later, we heard a jingling sound. It was the clink of the Bandit's boot buckles!

The sound stopped right in front of us.

"Sniff, snuff," muttered the Black

Bandit, his nose in the air. "You can't hide from me, my meaty little mice!" he meowed. I heard the clinking coming closer and closer. Then a frantic cry rang out.

"Your Excellency! We cannot find any pawprints!" a puzzled voice informed the **Bandit**.

"**Get a grip**, you nitwit! Do you think these mice have wings?" bawled the **Bandit**. "I don't care if you have to search every inch of this ship with your bare paws! Find those mice now!"

Then he headed down the hall.

SILVER UNDER
THE SUN

Once the **Black Bandit** had left, I ran back to our cell and leaned out the window. Down on the deck, the cats were racing around in circles, looking for us. Fur was flying everywhere!

"I think we need a new plan," I said. "Anyone have any ideas?"

"I have one!" Trap shrieked. "Let's go home!"

"But how are we going to get there?" Thea squeaked. "We can't swim. My pawstroke is awful!"

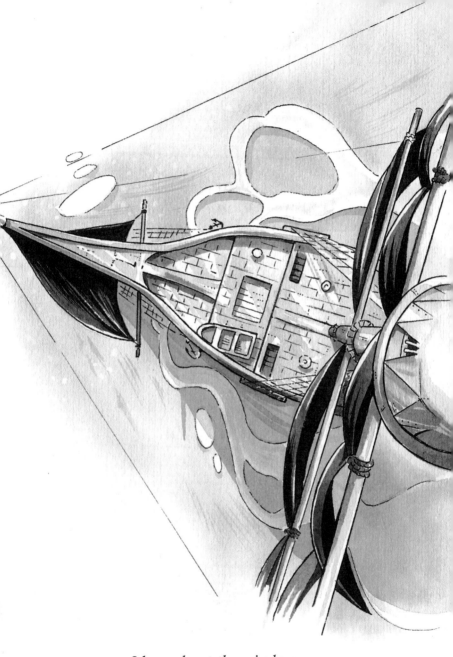

I leaned out the window.

I took out a pen and began to write:

1. *We had to cross the ocean to reach New Mouse City.*

2. *We could not swim home.*

3. *We had to force the cats to jump ship!*

I stared out over the pirate's ship, thinking. The silver deck gleamed brightly in the hot afternoon sun. A mouse could go blind looking at all that silver!

Just then, Trap rested his paw on the mast. "Yowee! This ship is as hot as a bed at the Fry Mouse Tanning Salon!"

I stared at him, eyes wide open. "That's it!" I squeaked. "I know exactly how we're going to get rid of the cats!"

LIKE A FRYING PAN

"This ship is made of metal. The silver is so hot it's burning up," I explained. "All we need to do is turn up the heat. At high noon tomorrow, we'll start a FIRE. The whole ship will get as hot as a frying pan. The cats will jump overboard, and the ship will be ours!"

Trap grinned. "I like it," he smirked. "We'll fry them up like catburgers at the Dog Heaven Grill!"

"But the Black Bandit will just get into a lifeboat," Thea observed.

I laughed. "That's the best part," I explained. "Their lifeboats are made of silver, too!"

Benjamin tugged at my jacket. "But, Uncle, what will happen to the cats? We can't let them DROWN!," he insisted.

He is such a tenderhearted mouslet.

HO-HUM ISLAND

Trap stared at my little nephew as if Benjamin had just stolen his last Cheesy Chew. "Little Mousey, who cares? They are cats!"

"I have an idea," Thea said. "Maybe there is an island nearby. When the cats jump ship, they can swim to the island. Let's go check out Tomcat Jack's maps."

I quickly leafed through my diary, searching for the plan of the ship. "There it is! Tomcat Jack's control room! Let's go!"

We RACED down the ship's silver hallways to the control room. In the center of the room stood a long silver table covered with strange seafaring gadgets, maps, and tools. I peered at a map of the ocean. "It looks like the nearest island is something called Ho-hum Island."

"There's nothing around that island. It's all *by itself*," Thea noted.

"Great!" cried Trap. "Those no-good cats will never be able to leave!"

"There's just one little problem," Thea said. "The Silver Claw is headed away from the island. If the pirates jump overboard tomorrow, they'll never be

able to swim there. We have to figure out a way to change the ship's course."

Suddenly, my sister pointed to a big compass in the middle of the room.

"Do you know how a compass works?" she asked. "The magnetic needle points to the north. But if you put a magnet near the compass, you can shift the needle."

I looked around. Nothing. "I'm afraid finding a magnet on this ship will be like searching for a whisker in a haystack!" I groaned.

THE LUCKY CHARM

Just then, Benjamin began squeaking. "I have a magnet, Uncle Geronimo!" he cried.

He proudly held up his lucky charm. It was a refrigerator magnet shaped like a small piece of cheese. I'm not sure why Benjamin thought the magnet was lucky, but he carried it with him everywhere. He brought it with him to Squeaking School, to the dentist, and even when he got his fur cut at Sniprat the Barber.

magnet

Thea stuck the lucky charm to the compass. Then she checked the needle.

"There!" she said, satisfied. "From now on, the compass will point toward Ho-hum Island!"

We decided to hide in a huge silver trunk filled with maps.

Seconds later, I heard a noise. I lifted the trunk's lid just enough to spot Tomcat Jack.

He took one look at the compass and began bouncing around like a basketball with whiskers.

Me eeeoOOooowwWWW!!!

"We are off course! Hurry, everybody to their posts!" he screeched.

ALL CATS AT THE READY!

Tomcat Jack quickly grabbed a silver megaphone and began shouting out orders.

"All cats at the ready! Hoist the jenny! Lower the flying jib! Tighten up that boom lift! Keep an eye on the topsail!"

Talon, the ship's officer, rushed over. "What's going on, Jack?" he cried. "Have you been eating catnip again? Why are we changing course?"

Tomcat Jack wiped the sweat from his

whiskers. He looked dazed and confused.

"I can't understand it," he muttered. "One minute we were sailing along just fine. The next minute we were headed in the wrong direction! But it's OK now. We're back on course."

I grinned and lowered the lid. Yes, we were back on course, all right. We were headed straight for Ho-hum Island!

COUNTDOWN:
THREE, TWO,
ONE . . .

By **eleven** the
next morning, we were
ready. We were also a little
squashed from spending
the night in the trunk.

Trap was so excited he
could hardly keep still.
"Can't wait to COOK those
cats!" he squeaked. "This is
better than the time I
cornered those ratburglars
with my electronic weed
whacker!"

We waited until we spotted Ho-hum Island. Then we quickly scampered into the powder room. No, this powder room wasn't for curling whiskers or fluffing up fur. It was filled with barrels of gunpowder!

Each one of us took a barrel of gunpowder and ran to our posts. Our plan was to confuse the pirates and make them believe that the whole ship was on fire. We would start **twelve** fires in **twelve** separate spots on the ship.

"**Three, two, one** . . . fire!"

With a crackling noise, flames licked the walls. Black smoke filled the air.

We heard the cats shouting: Fire! Fire! Fire!

Fire! Fire! Fire!

Fire! Fire! Fire!

The flames were spreading fast.

The flames were spreading fast, fanned by the wind off the ocean. We wrapped our paws with wet towels to keep from **BURNING**. The ship was getting hotter than the Cheeses of the World float at the Mousey's Day Parade! Meanwhile, the pirate cats were racing around in a panic.

We could hear them meowing.

Have we been attacked?

Did the kitchen blow up?

What happened?

I want my mommy!

By now, the ship was glowing from the heat. The cats were hopping around on the deck as if they were standing on the grill at Slinkrat's Sizzling Steak House!

After a while, the cats gave up the crazy dance moves and began to jump overboard.

"STOP, YOU SCOUNDRELS! ONLY I SAY WHEN IT IS TIME TO JUMP!" meowed a furious Black Bandit. But for once, no one was listening.

A RED-HOT CLAW

We waited for all of the pirates to get into the water. Then Trap and I ran to the sails, and Thea took the helm. Benjamin quickly closed the doors to the cabins that were on **FIRE**. He put some wet towels at the bottom of each door. Without any air, the **FLAMES** slowly began to go out.

When the pirates realized what had happened, they tried to climb back on board. But not one cat got a paw on deck. We had already raised the sails and were speeding away.

"WE'RE OFF TO NEW MOUSE CITY!!!" cried Trap, grinning from whisker to whisker.

I caught sight of the Black Bandit glaring back at us. The wind carried some of his words. "SOMEDAY we'll meet again, little micey!" he shrieked. "And when we do, you're going to wish you had never learned how to squeak!"

Then he cut the air with his sword, as if he were chopping us up.

Prowls was doing the kitty paddle, trying to keep up with his brother. We also spotted Slobbertooth, the chef; Claws, our friendly

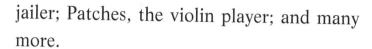

jailer; Patches, the violin player; and many more.

Thea leaned out of the boat to scan the horizon. Ho-hum Island was very close. Before long, the pirate cats gave up trying to follow us and began swimming toward it. **WE HEARD THEM SINGING AS THEY SWAM.** "Catchy," said my sister, tapping her paw to the beat. Then she grabbed a pencil and began jotting down the words to the song.

"*If you see a big ship on the water,*
Beware, the pirate cats are near!
If you see our tough fur and tails waving,
Beware, the pirate cats are here!
We are many, we are mean,
Always ready for the unforeseen,
Forever looking for great treasure,

Forget fighting, you just won't measure!
Meoooww . . . We're the mightiest cats
around,
So give us your gold, and don't make a
sound!"

Of course, we had to sing our own battle
song in reply.

"A THOUSAND TAILS RAISED IN THE AIR,
A THOUSAND VOICES SQUEAK WITH CARE,
RODENTS CHEER AND HEAVE A SIGH,
SWEET MOUSE ISLAND
WILL NEVER DIE!"

Cat-roast Surprise

The days went by. Each morning, I searched the sea for our precious Mouse Island. But so far, there was not an island or a mouse IN SIGHT. I was getting as homesick as a truckrat on a cross-country delivery. Boy, do I **HATE** traveling!

We had checked out the ship from top to bottom. Luckily, the supplies on board would last for at least a few years. We each chose a cabin to sleep in. I was sleeping in the Black Bandit's room. Benjamin insisted on staying with me. He wanted to have a sleepover party every night. "We can have pillow fights and sing songs and tell stories all night long! OK, Uncle?" he squeaked.

I was tired already. But I didn't have the heart to say no.

The **Bandit's** room was filled with some very strange things. I discovered a big black tarantula in a golden cage. It was the **Bandit's** pet. There was even a leash for her daily walk! In a small silver bowl was her favorite food: ant soup, fried flies, and mashed gnats. I bet Chef Slobbertooth had fun cooking that!

Besides the tarantula, I also found dozens of flowery homemade pillows. It seemed the

Black Bandit had a secret hobby: needlepoint! I smiled to myself. Now that the Bandit was stuck on Ho-hum Island, he'd have lots of time on his paws. Maybe he could needlepoint a pillow for each of the cats. He could hand them out as Christmas gifts.

I climbed into **bed**, avoiding the rug. It was made of soft gray fur. It might have been mouse fur. I tried not to think about it,

but it was hard. I could almost hear that poor rug squeak! On a bedside table sat a cup with a picture of a cat on it. I think it was Sir Catfish the Third, the first cat to sail around the world. I wonder if he'd had a mouse rug, too.

Thea had settled in Prowls's cabin. It was

filled with toys. There was a mouse marionette, a spinning top, lots of windup mice, and a furry cat-in-the-box that meowed when it popped open. On the shelf over the bed sat an old mechanical toy. It was a cat pulling a mouse's tail. The mouse looked like he'd been

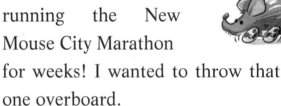

running the New Mouse City Marathon for weeks! I wanted to throw that one overboard.

Trap had chosen the cabin belonging to Chef Slobbertooth. The cabin was covered with grease stains. All kinds of cookbooks lined the shelves. I read a few of the titles.

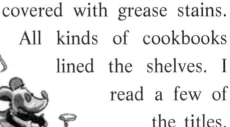

CATS IN THE KITCHEN: 50 WHISKER-LICKIN' MEALS IN MINUTES, THE HUNGRY CAT COOKS, and **HOW TO THROW THE PURRFECT DINNER PARTY.**

Trap sprawled out on Slobbertooth's leather love seat. "Hey, listen to this," he said, reading recipes from a note titled *Snails for Tails*.

Cat-roast Surprise: Roasted snails with potatoes

Crispy Cat's Cradle: Fried snails in a pastry shell

Hearty Cat Chowder: Snail soup with cream and vegetables

The Happy Cat Hoagie: Raw snail on a roll with oil and vinegar

THANK YOU, BLACK BANDIT!

I was at the helm when Benjamin came looking for me, waving a broom and a dust rag.

"**UNCLE** Geronimo, come and see what I found!" he called, tugging at my jacket.

He was dancing around like a kernel of popcorn before it pops! "Please, **UNCLE**! Right away to the cabin!" he squeaked.

"Cabin? What cabin?" I asked, confused. For a minute, I started thinking about an old log cabin we used to go to in the summers. It was right on beautiful Lake Lakelakelake.

"UNCLE GERONIMO," insisted Benjamin, interrupting my thoughts. "Guess what I found under the Black Bandit's bed!"

"Another tarantula?" I asked nervously.

"No!" squeaked my nephew. "A secret hiding place!"

Benjamin was right. Under the Bandit's bed was a trapdoor. It was chained shut with a huge silver lock.

"Hurry, let's open it!" said Trap. His eyes were as big as two saucers of milk.

"Let's not get too excited," I warned. "We don't want to be disappointed. It could just be the Bandit's dirty underwear!"

Half an hour later, we finally broke the

lock. And I was wrong. There was no underwear in this hiding place.

"TREASURE!"

cried Trap, diving into a mountain of gold and silver coins. Precious stones and glittering jewels spilled onto the floor. It was an amazing sight!

Trap put a crown on his head and took a bow. "How do I look? Like the **King of the Pi-rats?**" he squeaked, grinning.

"**Wow!** Take a look at these rubies. They are as big as eggs!" called Benjamin. He held up two enormous gemstones.

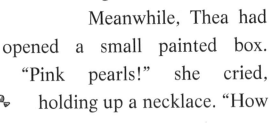

Meanwhile, Thea had opened a small painted box. "Pink pearls!" she cried, holding up a necklace. "How beautiful!" She fastened the strand around her neck. Then she stared at herself in a mirror. "They are *so* me!" she announced, beaming at her reflection.

"How beautiful!"

Also in the box was a bracelet, a ring, a pair of earrings, and a dazzling gold crown. I stared at the jewels. They looked so familiar. Suddenly, I slapped my forehead with my paw. "That's it!" I yelled. "I know where I have seen these jewels. Queen Natasha Noblesnout is wearing them in that famouse painting!"

I picked up a gold coin. It belonged to the Kingdom of Cats. Carved on one side was the pirates' motto: **What's Yours**

Queen
Noblesnout

Is Mine, What's Mine Is Mine!
(Someone really needed to teach these cats
a lesson in sharing.)

Then I spotted a silver coin. My eyes
opened wide. My fur stood on end. My heart
beat so fast I felt like I had just swum ten
laps in the pool at WaterRat Park.

This was not just any old silver coin. I cleaned my glasses so I could see it better.

"Moldy mozzarella!" I cried. "This is the legendary silver quarter! It was the first coin ever minted on Mouse Island!" I held the coin out so the others could see. The quarter was dated 1458. Mouse Island's motto was carved on the back:

Rodents Be Smart, Follow Your Heart!

STERN WIND!

"RODENTS BE SMART, FOLLOW YOUR HEART!" we chanted as we took turns at the helm. A stern wind pushed us home.

Yes, if this **wind kept up** we'd be sailing into Mouse Island in two shakes of a rat's tail. I was so happy! I couldn't wait to sink

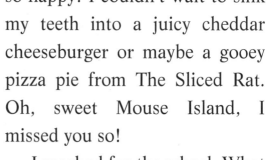

my teeth into a juicy cheddar cheeseburger or maybe a gooey pizza pie from The Sliced Rat. Oh, sweet Mouse Island, I missed you so!

I reached for the wheel. What a great ship! A real battleship. I wondered how many fights it had been through. Some sailors believe that ships have a soul. I bet this ship's **soul** was as rotten as a sewer rat.

Keeping an eye on the waves, *I was soon lost in my thoughts.* I wondered if anyone had taken the time to dust my aged cheese collection. Or my priceless set of the *Encyclopaedia Ratannica.*

I patted the notebook in my pocket. All my book needed now was an ending. I hoped it would be a happy one.

"Laaaaaaaaaand hoooooo!" came Trap's shout.

I snapped to attention.

"Land?" asked Thea, racing across the deck.

"Land, land, laaand!" sang Benjamin, kicking up his paws.

Thea twirled around in circles. "Home sweet home!" she sang. Trap played air guitar with his tail.

I guess we all looked pretty silly. We were dressed in the pirate cats' clothing. My sister had used her sewing skills to make them **smaller**.

Trap was wearing a big lacy shirt with lots of ruffles. He looked like the mouse from the high-wire act at the Big Cheese Circus.

Thea had on a yellow silk vest and the pearls she had found. Benjamin's oversized **red-and-white-striped** shirt made him look like a jailmouse.

As for me, I was wearing one of the

Black Bandit's coats. It was so long I swept the floor as I walked.

I tried to untangle my knotted whiskers. It was no use. They were wound up tighter than a spring. Next, I tried to smooth out my shirt. It was still a wrinkled mess.

"Don't worry about the look, Cousinkins!" squeaked Trap. He strutted around, puffing up his fur. "We're too good for any dress code! After all, it's not every mouse who can say he fought against pirates. Giant **pirate cats** as big as buildings!"

Thea giggled. "Let's not overdo it. I was there, too, you know," she replied.

"Are you calling me a liar?" Trap demanded, paws on his hips. "They WERE humongous cats. Don't you remember their claws? They were sharp enough to slice ten mice in half!" he insisted.

Thea made a
face at him.

"Well, maybe
not ten mice,"
Trap added. "Maybe
just **two**."

My sister rolled her eyes.

"OK, OK, maybe they
could just chop off some
fur," Trap admitted.
"But they were still the
BIGGEST cats
I have ever seen!"

Thea burst out laughing. "Why, of course
they were, Cousin," she said. "They were
also the *only* cats you have ever seen!"

SWEET, SWEET MOUSE ISLAND!

Can a land be sweet? I don't mean sweet like sugar on a cream-cheese doughnut. I mean sweet as in "melt your heart sweet." Yes, there was no other place like sweet, sweet Mouse Island. We sailed toward land, grinning from ear to ear. Our smiles were so wide we could have been poster mice for Flossy, my dental rat.

It felt so good to be home at last! By now you know how much I **HATE** traveling! We sailed by the statue that stands at the entrance to New Mouse City Harbor. It is the Statue of Liberty, holding **up** a big piece of

cheese. Mice come from all over just to see her. Today a crowd of rodents had gathered at her feet. They all gave us puzzled stares as we sailed by.

"Let's show those mice a real pirate's homecoming!" Trap shOUTed.

We bowed low. Then we waved our hats and cheered, "Hooray for New Mouse City!"

Next, before we could stop him, Trap fired a round from our ship's one hundred cannons. Luckily, the mice below knew it was only meant as a greeting. Leave it to my cousin to come in with a bang!

The other ships in the water quickly let us pass. Then they followed behind us in a line. It was like we were leading a floating mouse parade.

"**We are going to be famous, ratlets!**" cried Trap. He was *waving to the mice below* as if he were a famouse rock star or a big-time movie mouse. "Look at them!" he squeaked excitedly. "They're practically drooling over us! Wait until they see the treasure!"

We lowered the sails. The Silver Claw dropped anchor right in the middle of the harbor.

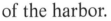

The four of us climbed into a rowboat and reached the shore. The crowd was extra noisy. They had enough questions to sink our ship!

"Where do you come from? And where does that enormouse ship come from?"

"Why the cannons? And what about that flag with the skull?"

"Look at their clothing! Hey, isn't that *Geronimo Stilton*, the newspaper mouse? You know, the one who published the YELLOW PAGES? Remember all those wrong numbers?"

Oops! I had forgotten all about the phone book disaster.

ALL IS FORGIVEN!

Fortunately, I didn't have to worry about the phone books. Now everyone just wanted to hear about our adventure. We told our tale on the WRAT radio program. We even appeared on Ben Squeaker's TV talk show.

We had become the island's national heroes! Not only because we had beaten the **pirate cats** and sent them to Ho-hum Island, but also because of that famouse silver quarter. It had been stolen by the pirates at the time of the Great Cat War!

As for the pirate ship, we finally agreed to give it to the city. The mayor ended up turning it into a mouseum dedicated to the history of rodents.

Now that we were famouse, my little mix-up with the YELLOW PAGES was forgiven. Once in a while, a rodent would call the office to place an order for some Furry Tails toilet paper. But I didn't mind. I was too busy working on my own paper. The paper in my notebook, that is. I buried myself behind

my desk and began writing my book. I wrote about our crazy balloon ride. I wrote about our capture by the **Black Bandit**. I wrote about our daring escape. *I even wrote about Chef Slobbertooth and the snails!*

The book was ready in less than a month. I had already chosen the title: **ATTACK OF THE BANDIT CATS**. I had a bestseller in the making. I could smell it! It was as strong as my great-grandma Scamper's garlic cheese rolls!

I had a bestseller in the making. I could smell it!

ISLANDS, PIZZAS, AND SUITCASES

Now, you are probably wondering what happened to all of the treasure. Well, each one of us used it in a different way. My sister bought a small island north of New Mouse City. She called it Thea's Wild Paradise. She goes there to vacation and to get away from the rat race. My sister also managed to sell the pirate cats' song to

a big-time record company. Believe it or not, that meow music is now at the **TOP OF THE CHARTS!** My sister still can't carry a tune, but she's singing all the way to the bank!

What did my cousin Trap do with his share of the treasure? Well, he built an **ENORMOUSE PIZZA RESTAURANT** shaped just like a pirate's ship. The waiters dress as pirates and serve HOT, STEAMING pizzas with evil names like the THIN CRUST SCREAM SUPREME. The place is a huge success. Mice are just scurrying to get in. Plus, they all want to meet Trap. Yes, my cousin is famouse — and not just because of our adventure. He's the star of his own television commercial. He swings back and forth on a rope with a hot slice of pizza between his teeth. "Come and see me at The Pirate's Ship for the very best pizzas in town!" he squeaks.

As for me and Benjamin, we came up with a different plan. A special plan. An unbelievably exciting plan! Right now, I am packing my suitcases for our trip. That's right, Benjamin and I have decided to travel around the world!

Yes, I have discovered that traveling really isn't so bad after all. In fact, I think every mouse should try it. Maybe my next book will be a travel guide: *Geronimo Stilton's Travel Tips for Tails of All Ages.* Hmm . . . that's not bad. I think I just might smell **MY NEXT BESTSELLER!**

Benjamin and I have decided to travel around the world.

Want to read my next adventure?
It's sure to be a fur-raising experience!

A Fabumouse Vacation for Geronimo

Sometimes a busy businessmouse like me needs a nice, relaxing vacation. But of all the rotten rats' luck — every time I tried to get away, disaster struck! By the time I finally tore myself away from *The Rodent's Gazette*, all the good trips were booked up. I found myself stuck in a flea-ridden old hotel, sharing a room with a bunch of Gerbil Scouts! I couldn't wait to get back to my comfy mouse hole in New Mouse City....

Don't miss any of my
fabumouse adventures!

www.geronimostilton.com/uk

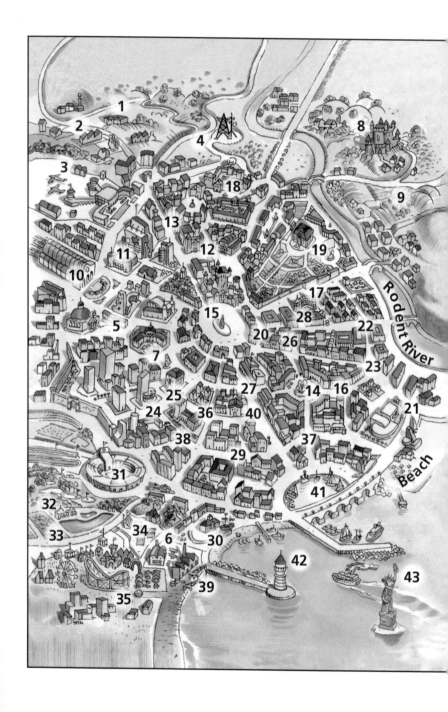

Map of New Mouse City

1. Industrial Zone
2. Cheese Factories
3. Angorat International Airport
4. WRAT Radio and Television Station
5. Cheese Market
6. Fish Market
7. Town Hall
8. Snotnose Castle
9. The Seven Hills of Mouse Island
10. Mouse Central Station
11. Trade Center
12. Movie Theater
13. Gym
14. Catnegie Hall
15. Singing Stone Plaza
16. The Gouda Theater
17. Grand Hotel
18. Mouse General Hospital
19. Botanical Gardens
20. Cheap Junk for Less (Trap's store)
21. Parking Lot
22. Museum of Modern Art
23. University and Library
24. *The Daily Rat*
25. *The Rodent's Gazette*
26. Trap's House
27. Fashion District
28. The Mouse House Restaurant
29. Environmental Protection Center
30. Harbor Office
31. Mousidon Square Garden
32. Golf Course
33. Swimming Pool
34. Blushing Meadow Tennis Courts
35. Curlyfur Island Amusement Park
36. Geronimo's House
37. New Mouse City Historic District
38. Public Library
39. Shipyard
40. Thea's House
41. New Mouse Harbor
42. Luna Lighthouse
43. The Statue of Liberty

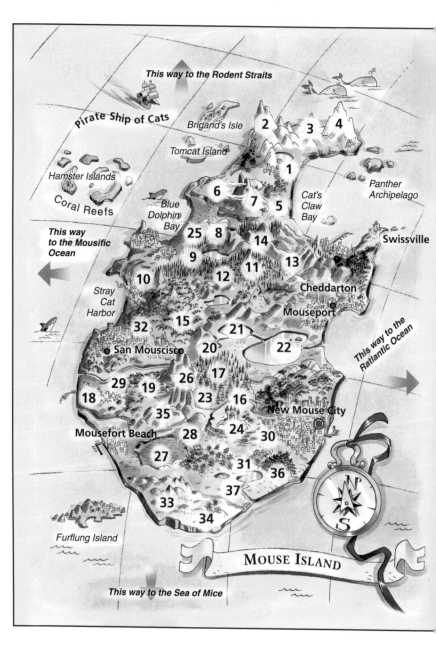

This way to the Rodent Straits

Pirate Ship of Cats

Brigand's Isle

Tomcat Island

Hamster Islands

Coral Reefs

Blue Dolphin Bay

This way to the Mousific Ocean

Stray Cat Harbor

San Mouscisco

Mousefort Beach

Furflung Island

This way to the Sea of Mice

Panther Archipelago

Cat's Claw Bay

Swissville

Cheddarton

Mouseport

This way to the Ratlantic Ocean

New Mouse City

MOUSE ISLAND

Map of Mouse Island

1. Big Ice Lake
2. Frozen Fur Peak
3. Slipperyslopes Glacier
4. Coldcreeps Peak
5. Ratzikistan
6. Transratania
7. Mount Vamp
8. Roastedrat Volcano
9. Brimstone Lake
10. Poopedcat Pass
11. Stinko Peak
12. Dark Forest
13. Vain Vampires Valley
14. Goose Bumps Gorge
15. The Shadow Line Pass
16. Penny Pincher Lodge
17. Nature Reserve Park
18. Las Ratayas Marinas
19. Fossil Forest
20. Lake Lake
21. Lake Lake Lake
22. Lake Lakelakelake
23. Cheddar Crag
24. Cannycat Castle
25. Valley of the Giant Sequoia
26. Cheddar Springs
27. Sulfurous Swamp
28. Old Reliable Geyser
29. Vole Vail
30. Ravingrat Ravine
31. Gnat Marshes
32. Munster Highlands
33. Mousehara Desert
34. Oasis of the Sweaty Camel
35. Cabbagehead Hill
36. Tropical Jungle
37. Rio Mosquito

Dear mouse friends,
thanks for reading, and farewell
till the next book.
It'll be another whisker-licking-good
adventure, and that's a promise!

Geronimo Stilton